An I Can Read Book®

BUZBY
to the
RESCUE

by Julia Hoban
Pictures by John Himmelman

P9-DHG-487

HarperTrophy
A Division of HarperCollinsPublishers

I Can Read Book is a registered trademark of HarperCollins Publishers.
Buzby to the Rescue
Text copyright © 1993 by Julia Hoban
Illustrations copyright © 1993 by John Himmelman
Printed in the U.S.A. All rights reserved.

Library of Congress Cataloging-in-Publication Data
Hoban, Julia.
  Buzby to the rescue / by Julia Hoban ; pictures by John Himmelman.
     p.   cm.—(An I can read book)
  Summary: Buzby the hotel cat does his best to help visiting movie star
Serena Lovejoy keep track of her jewels and enjoy her stay at the hotel.
  ISBN 0-06-021025-7. — ISBN 0-06-021024-9 (lib. bdg.)
  ISBN 0-06-444184-9 (pbk.)
  [1. Cats—Fiction. 2. Hotels, motels, etc.—Fiction.] I. Himmelman,
John, ill. II. Title. III. Series.
PZ7.H63487Bud   1993   91-46085
[E]—dc20   CIP
                                               AC

Typography by Daniel C. O'Leary
❖
First Harper Trophy edition, 1995.

For H,

P.R.H.

—J. Hoban

For Dale Payson

—J. Himmelman

Buzby was a hotel cat.

He wore a bright blue uniform

with big brass buttons.

Buzby liked to ride
the hotel elevators.

He liked the desserts

that the cook made for him.

Most of all

Buzby liked to meet

the hotel guests.

One day the hotel manager said,

"Buzby, Serena Lovejoy

is coming to stay.

She is a big movie star.

Take special care of her."

"Yes, sir!" Buzby said,

and twitched his whiskers.

Buzby took his place

at the hotel entrance.

A big car drove up.

Out stepped Serena Lovejoy.

"Miss Lovejoy," said Buzby,

"my name is Buzby.

I am here to help you."

11

"What a sweet pussycat,"

said Miss Lovejoy.

"You can carry my bags,

but I always carry my jewelry case.

I want to be sure

it will be safe.

"Here is my hatbox,

my suitcase, and . . .

MERCY!

WHERE IS MY JEWELRY CASE?"

"You are holding it, Miss Lovejoy,"
Buzby said.

"Oh, how silly of me,"
said Miss Lovejoy.

"Thank you, Frisbee."

"My name is Buzby," said Buzby,

and he picked up

Miss Lovejoy's suitcases.

"Miss Lovejoy," said the manager,

"let me put your jewels

in the hotel safe."

"Oh, no!" said Miss Lovejoy.

"I want my pearls, my diamonds,

and my royal ruby with me

at all times."

"But Miss Lovejoy," said Buzby,

"your jewels will be safer with us."

"No, no, Bugsy,"

said Miss Lovejoy.

"My name is Buzby," said Buzby.

"Miss Lovejoy," said the manager,

"you have forgotten

the key to your room."

"Oh, how silly of me,"

said Miss Lovejoy,

and she went up to her room.

Buzby went back to his place
at the hotel door.
Two guests arrived.

"Is Serena Lovejoy staying here?"

one of them asked Buzby.

"Yes, she is," said Buzby.

"Then we will stay here too,"

the guest said.

"Wait a minute, Charlie,"

said the other one.

"How are we going to get it?"

"Don't worry, Louie,"

said Charlie.

"It will be easy."

"This does not sound good,"

Buzby said to himself.

"I must keep an eye on them."

Charlie and Louie

went into the dining room.

Buzby followed.

Charlie and Louie ate dinner.

Buzby watched.

"I want to get it now!"

said Charlie.

"Okay," said Louie.

"Let's find Miss Lovejoy's room."

They finished eating

and got into the elevator.

28

"Wait!" cried Buzby.

The elevator doors closed.

"I must follow them," said Buzby.

Buzby ran up the stairs.

Suddenly he heard

"MERCY, MY ROYAL RUBY!"

He saw Charlie and Louie

running away

from Miss Lovejoy's room.

"Stop!" shouted Buzby.

Charlie and Louie

ran down the stairs.

Buzby ran after them.

Charlie and Louie

ran toward the revolving doors.

Just as Buzby

got to the bottom of the stairs,

a waiter came out

of the dining room.

He was pushing a cart

filled with desserts.

34

CRASH!

Buzby ran into the cart.

PLOP!

He fell in some banana cream pie.

Buzby tried to stand up,

but he slipped on some ice cream.

ZOOM!

Buzby slid through

the revolving doors.

BANG!

Charlie and Louie went spinning
back into the lobby.

WHUMP!

Buzby fell on top of them.

"Help! There is a banana cream cat on top of me," said Louie.

Suddenly Serena Lovejoy

ran into the lobby.

"MY RUBY HAS BEEN STOLEN!"

she cried.

"Don't worry, Miss Lovejoy,"

said Buzby.

"I have caught the robbers."

"We are not robbers," said Charlie.

"Empty your pockets," said Buzby.

Charlie and Louie

emptied their pockets.

Out fell two pens, some paper,

and a picture of Miss Lovejoy,

but no ruby.

"We just wanted

Miss Lovejoy's autograph,"

said Charlie.

44

"I want my ruby back!"

Miss Lovejoy cried.

"This is the worst hotel

in the world!"

"Don't cry," said Buzby.

"I will find your ruby."

"If you find my ruby,"

said Miss Lovejoy,

"I will give you a reward."

"Wait here," said Buzby.

"I will be back with your ruby."

Buzby went to Miss Lovejoy's room.

He jumped on the dressing table.

CRASH!

His tail knocked over a jar.

"What a mess," said Buzby.

"I should clean it up."

Buzby looked at the jar.

It said COLD CREAM.

"I love cream," he said.

"I will lick it up!"

Buzby started to lick

the cold cream.

"Ugh!" said Buzby.

"This tastes awful!"

Then he looked at the cream.
There was a bright red cherry
in the middle of it.

"Maybe the cherry

will taste better," said Buzby.

"Ouch! This is not a cherry!"

Just then the manager,

Miss Lovejoy, and Charlie and Louie

ran into the room.

"You found my royal ruby!"

cried Miss Lovejoy.

"It was in the cold cream,"

said Buzby.

"How silly of me,"

said Miss Lovejoy.

"I must have put it there

to keep it safe.

Thank you, Mugsy."

"My name is Buzby," said Buzby.

"This is the best hotel

in the world," cried Miss Lovejoy,

"and you are the sweetest pussycat."

She kissed Buzby.

"You can have any reward you want."

"Well," said Buzby,

"I do like cream."

"You shall have

as much as you want,"

said Miss Lovejoy.

"Miss Lovejoy," said Charlie,

"may we have your autograph?"

"Of course," said Miss Lovejoy.

Miss Lovejoy was happy.

She had her royal ruby.

Charlie and Louie were happy.

They had Miss Lovejoy's autograph.

The manager was happy.

He had the best hotel in the world.

But Buzby was happiest of all.

Every morning

a big bottle of fresh cream

was delivered to the hotel door

with a note.

It said:

To Buzby,
the best hotel
cat in the
world!

Serena Lovejoy